My Mommy Is Magic

Dawn Richards ★ Jane Massey

BARRON'S

First edition for the United States and Canada published in 2015 by Barron's Educational Series, Inc.

First published in Great Britain in 2013 by Picture Corgi, an imprint of Random House Children's Publishers UK, A Random House Group Company, 61–63 Uxbridge Road, London W5 5SA Great Britain

Text copyright © Random House Children's Publishers UK, 2014
Illustrations copyright © Jane Massey, 2014. The right of Jane Massey to be identified as the illustrator of this work has been asserted in accordance with the Copyright, Designs and Patents Act 1988.

All inquiries should be addressed to:
Barron's Educational Series, Inc.
250 Wireless Boulevard, Hauppauge, New York 11788
www.barronseduc.com

ISBN: 978-0-7641-6757-7

Library of Congress Control Number: 2014947898

Printed in China

Date of Manufacture: December 2014

Manufactured by: Toppan Leefung Printing, Ltd., Dongguan, China

9 8 7 6 5 4 3 2 1

I think my mommy is **magic** –
I notice every day . . .

. . . that whenever **magic** happens,
Mommy's never far away.

I think
my mommy is
magic!

I'm sure it must be true . . .

Sometimes I can't believe
the many magic things we do!

My mommy
knows just
what I like,

she knows
just what
to say.

And if I hurt myself . . .

. . . my mommy **magics** it away!

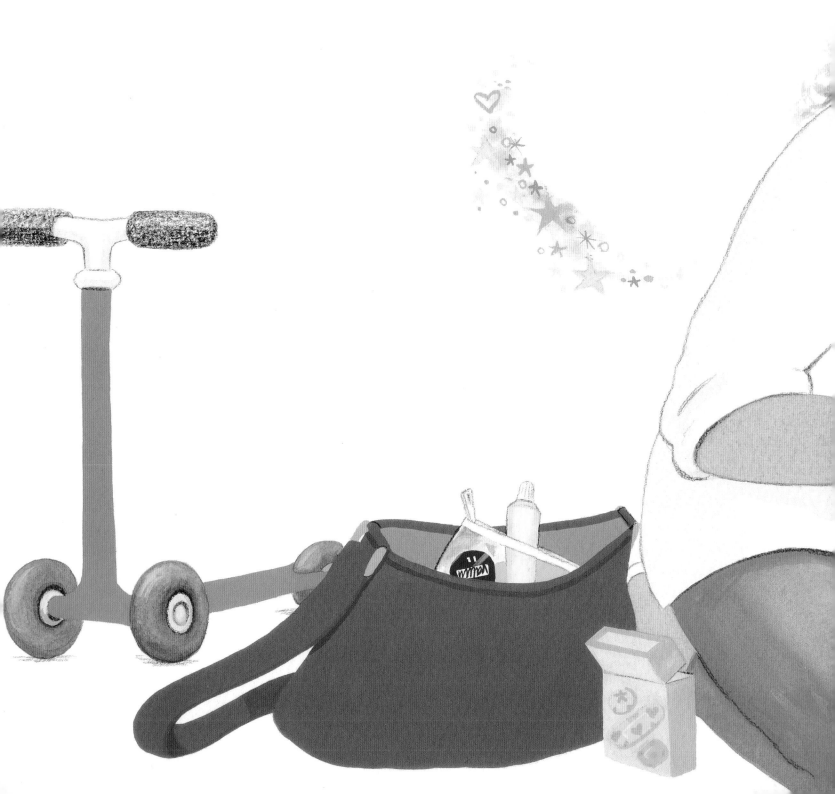

I think my mommy is magic –
and everybody knows.

They need my mommy's magic,
and so off to work she goes.

There are times I really miss her,

and I wish that she would stay . . .

. . . but just like **magic**, soon she's back,
as though she never went away!

My mommy is a super cook and all her food tastes yummy.

She makes delicious puddings
that do magic in my tummy!

Even when I'm grumpy,
and it's time to have a bath,

my magic mommy
knows just how to make
me smile and laugh.

My mommy MUST be magic,
the stories that she tells . . .

Little Red
Riding Hood

. . . come straight to life
– it feels as though she's
casting magic spells.

My mommy
must be magic,
because when it's
time for bed

she gives me hugs and then a
magic kiss upon my head.

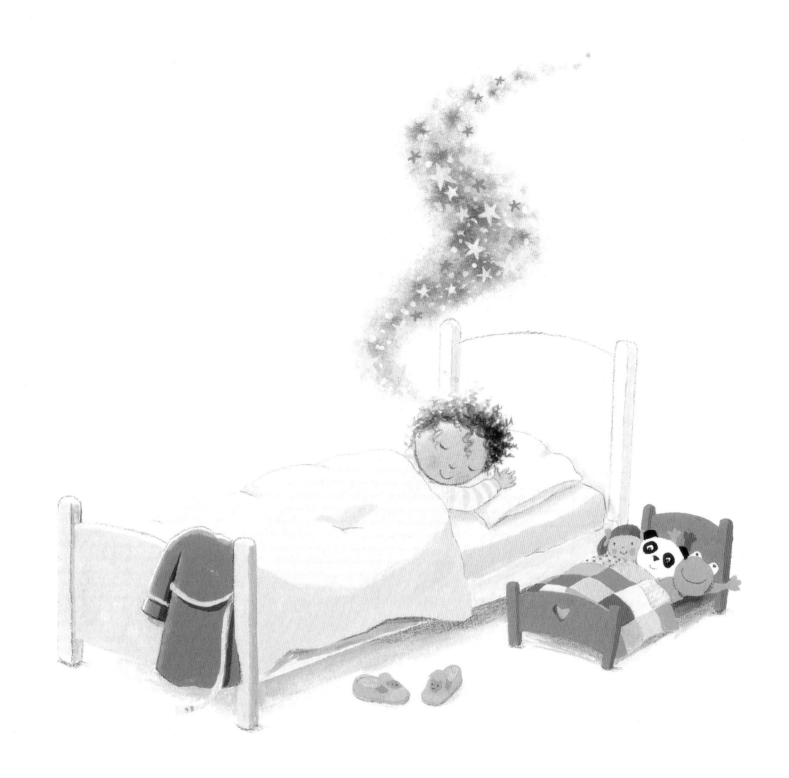

And in my dreamy magic sleep,
one thing I know for sure . . .

when I wake up, my magic mom
will love me even more!

I KNOW my mom is magic . . .

I know she has to be . . .